— Bats in the Schoolhouse

BABY BATS
DON'T HATCH FROM EGGS

BY DARLENE HARTFORD

Illustrated by Matt Hebb

 **FriesenPress**

Suite 300 - 990 Fort St
Victoria, BC, Canada, V8V 3K2
www.friesenpress.com

ISBN
978-1-4602-5155-3 (Paperback)
978-1-4602-5156-0 (eBook)

1. *Juvenile Fiction, Animals*

Distributed to the trade by The Ingram Book Company

Dedicated to
Maisy and Tavin

"Faster, Mommy, faster!" squealed Sebastian as he hung on tightly under his mother's wing. Sebastian loved flying as fast as his mother's wings would take them. Sebastian was a **NEWBORN BAT PUP** who lived in the attic of the old yellow schoolhouse.

During the day, Sebastian snuggled in his mother's soft fur and slept under her strong **LEATHERY** wing. When the golden sun set and the silver moon rose, Mother Bat would fly out of the attic to feed on tasty bugs. Sebastian was left in the roost with the other newborns, and a babysitter, until Mother Bat returned to feed him.

"I can't wait until I'm big enough to fly by myself," yearned Sebastian as he watched his mother fly off.

Mother Bat, knowing how eager Sebastian was to fly, took her newborn out of the roost one special night. That was a night Sebastian would **NEVER FORGET!**

Together they flew over the forest and ponds, but when Mother Bat swooped down to drink from Swanson Pond, she saw Spotted Owl flying towards them. That was not good because **SPOTTED OWL** was a dangerous predator!

"Hold on tight, Sebastian!" squealed Mother Bat as she circled into the forest. She fled from Spotted Owl, but he was swift, and was soon upon her. He **CHASED** her through the woods, over the pond, and under the bridge. Spotted Owl was **MASSIVE**, strong and fast, and was getting much **TOO** close!

Mother Bat worried Sebastian might fall off during her quick turns. She swooped down to the forest floor, gently laying him on a log, under a leaf. Then she quickly **ZIG-ZAGGED** throughout the forest, tricking Spotted Owl as she lured him away from Sebastian.

Spotted Owl soon tired of chasing Mother Bat. He flew to his perch, high in a tree, and **HOOTED** with a huff, "You're a lucky little bat tonight!"

Unfortunately, Spotted Owl's perch was right above Sebastian's hiding spot. Mother Bat nervously hid in a tree nearby. She **WAITED** for Spotted Owl to fly off, but to no avail—he stayed, ruffled his feathers, and went to sleep.

Night passed, and the silver moon **DISAPPEARED** as the golden sun began to rise. It wasn't safe for Mother Bat to fly in the daylight with Spotted Owl so close. She sighed deeply, hoping that Sebastian would be **SAFE** in the forest, and she eventually went to sleep.

Sebastian was frightened and cold on the log below. He knew something was wrong, so he stayed very still under the leaf and wished he were **SAFELY** snuggled in Mother Bat's fur. Sebastian rolled over and tried to get warm. Much to his surprise, he **FELL OFF** the log and landed in something soft and warm. It felt like Mother Bat's fur, but it wasn't fur—it was a bed filled with **FEATHERS**. Sebastian also felt some hard, round things that made funny **CRACKING** noises. He'd never seen or heard anything like that in his roost.

Sebastian didn't realize that he'd fallen into the nest of Nellie, a beautiful **CANADA GOOSE.** And Sebastian also didn't know it was a very special day for Nellie at Swanson Pond. On this day, Nellie's **EGGS** were going to **HATCH**, and she was very excited.

Sebastian snuggled under Nellie's warm down feathers and rolled into a piece of broken eggshell left by a **GOSLING** hatching through its shell. The eggshell felt just like Mother Bat's wings hugging him! Finally, Sebastian felt **WARM, COZY**, and **SAFE.** Soon he was fast asleep in Nellie's soft, comfortable nest.

Nellie felt movement in her nest and quickly stepped out, expecting to see a baby **GOSLING**. But instead, Nellie saw only a few broken shells. No goslings had fully hatched.

Then Nellie saw Sebastian. She was **STARTLED**, confused, and became **FRANTIC**, honking and circling her nest.

"What is in my nest?" squawked Nellie. "It looks like a **BABY BAT**! How can this be? **OH NO**—did I hatch a baby bat? Yes, I HAVE hatched a baby bat! Here it is, inside my nest!"

Nellie was puzzled and very **UPSET**. But as upset as she was, Nellie knew she must **SIT** on her eggs and keep them warm before her goslings would hatch. All day Nellie sat on the nest, worried she might hatch another baby bat. As a matter of fact, Nellie was so worried that she **HONKED**, squawked, and **FUSSED** all day long.

At the end of the day, George Gander finally went to Nellie and asked, "Why all the **HONKING** and **SQUAWKING** all day, Nellie? What is wrong?"

"I'm honking and squawking because I've **HATCHED** a baby bat!" Nellie cried out to George.

"Nellie, you silly goose," said George, "Goslings and ducklings hatch from eggs, but baby bats **DON'T** hatch from eggs." Then George casually waddled off to enjoy his evening swim on Swanson Pond.

Nellie's friends, Tasha Turtle and Daphne Dragonfly, also heard her squawking and honking. They went to Nellie's nest and asked, "What's wrong, Nellie? Why all the honking and squawking?"

Nellie honked desperately while telling her friends that she'd **HATCHED** a baby bat.

The two looked at each other with **ASTONISHMENT.**

"Nellie...goslings, ducklings, and my cute babies hatch from eggs," explained Tasha.

"My beautiful dragonflies, and even spiders, hatch from eggs," added Daphne.

"But baby bats do **NOT**, you silly goose!" **WAILED** the two in unison.

Disgruntled, Nellie stepped off her nest to show her friends the **PESKY** little bat she'd hatched.

There in the nest was Sebastian. He comfortably stretched his wings and wiggled his little legs from his **COZY** place inside the eggshell.

The three friends moved closer, peering into the eggshell.

Suddenly Sebastian felt uncomfortable. Was he being **GLARED** at?

Sebastian opened his eyes. Looking back at him were two angry black eyes, an **ENORMOUS** beak, a **BULBOUS** green head with two bulging eyes, and four blue-bladed wings **FRANTICALLY** buzzing!

Sebastian squealed out in fright! But no one heard his **HIGH-PITCH SQUEAL**—no one except Mother Bat.

Nellie, Tasha, and Daphne were shocked when that little speck of a bat opened his mouth, showing **POINTY** white teeth. They stepped back quickly and stared at each other in disbelief!

Upon hearing Sebastian's frantic **SQUEAL**, Mother Bat swooped down to Nellie's nest, tucked Sebastian under her wing, and flew back to safety at the top of the tree.

Mother Bat was so quick that Nellie, Tasha, and Daphne were **BEWILDERED**.

"What was that?" the three **CRIED** out.

Tasha

Turtle quickly tucked into her shell. Daphne Dragonfly flew off in a blaze of blue. Nellie flapped her great wings, **SQUAWKING** even louder.

And then, nervously, Nellie checked her eggs and looked inside the broken eggshell. With relief she found her eggs were safe, and that **BOTHERSOME** little bat was gone. **FINALLY**, Nellie stopped squawking!

As Nellie fluffed her feathers and settled into her nest, Mother Bat gently **FOLDED** her wings around Sebastian, calling out, "Thank-you for watching my baby all day. Spotted Owl **CHASED** us last night. I was frightened and hid my pup in the forest, and couldn't **SAFELY** fetch him."

"**OH!**" exclaimed Nellie with surprise, "**I** didn't hatch that baby bat?"

Mother Bat was confused and squealed, "Of course not, you **SILLY** goose. Baby bats don't hatch from eggs!"

Before returning to the roost that night, Mother Bat watched Nellie, the beautiful Canada Goose, as she **CRADLED** her new goslings. As Mother Bat flew closer, she heard one gosling sweetly honk, "Mother, where's my baby bat **BROTHER?**"

Nellie lovingly said, "That wasn't your brother, you silly little goose. Baby bats **DON'T** hatch from eggs!"

Then, in the light of the silver moon, Mother Bat smiled **AS MOTHERS DO**, and flew back to the **SCHOOLHOUSE** with Sebastian tucked safely under wing.

BAT FACTS

Newborn bat pups are the size of a
man's **THUMBNAIL**.

Bats are mammals. Baby bats are born alive and
feed on their mother's milk.

Nursing females really do leave their newborns with a
"BABYSITTER BAT" when feeding at night!

Pups fly with their mothers for three weeks, holding
on under mother's wing.

Pups learn to fly **ALONE** between three and
four weeks of age.

ABOUT THE AUTHOR

Darlene Hartford lives in Peachland, British Columbia with her husband. She enjoys an Okanagan lifestyle residing on Lake Okanagan, surrounded by nature. The series, Bats in the Schoolhouse Attic, includes her first published manuscripts, fulfilling a lifelong dream of writing children's books.

The lakefront community of Peachland has 5,000 residents, as well as a colony of 2,000 bats, that live in a historic schoolhouse. The school was closed and boarded shut for ten years, but with the decision to preserve the building, the bat colony was also saved. A community educational program was established to promote public awareness of the value of bats, and to discredit myths surrounding the protected species. Darlene Hartford is the Peachland Chamber of Commerce Director of Peachland Bats Educational and Conservation Program.

The colony of winged mammals inspired Darlene Hartford to write a series of whimsical stories with endearing bat characters. The Peachland Historic Primary School is home to a maternity colony, consisting of mainly female bats, roosting together, producing offspring. The stories are adventures of mother bats with their pups, and provide a harmonious balance between the imaginative and the educational. Each book provides Bat Facts in reference to the storyline.

Darlene Hartford dedicated the series, Bats in the Schoolhouse Attic, to her seven grandchildren.

CPSIA information can be obtained
at www.ICGtesting.com
Printed in the USA
LVIC06n2039090315
429850LV00005B/7

* 9 7 8 1 4 6 0 2 5 1 5 5 3 *